HODDER CHILDREN'S BOOKS

First published in Great Britain in 2019
by Hodder and Stoughton

Text © Nadiya Hussain 2019
Illustrations © Ella Bailey 2019

A CIP catalogue record of this book
is available from the British Library.

HB ISBN: 978 1 444 94643 7
PB ISBN: 978 1 444 94644 4

10 9 8 7 6 5 4 3 2 1

Printed and bound in China.

MIX
Paper from
responsible sources
FSC® C104740
www.fsc.org

Hodder Children's Books
An imprint of
Hachette Children's Group
Part of Hodder and Stoughton
Carmelite House
50 Victoria Embankment
London, EC4Y 0DZ

An Hachette UK Company
www.hachette.co.uk

www.hachettechildrens.co.uk

My Monster and Me

Written by

Nadiya Hussain

Illustrated by

Ella Bailey

Hodder Children's Books

This is my monster.

And this is me.

I've always known my monster.

It's always been there.

It knows **ALL** about me.

Maybe my monster arrived when I did.

Maybe it moved in when I learned to walk and talk.
I don't remember.

It was always **BIG**.
When it stood in front of me,
I could see nothing but its huge tummy.

At night, when I lay in bed, I could hear nothing but its **ginormous, growly** snore.

I wanted Mum to take it away.
But when Mum was there,
my monster hid.

I wished my brother
could take it away. But
my monster hid again.

I wanted Dad to take it away.
But it hid from him, too.

My monster got **bossier!**
It started telling me what to do
when I was getting dressed,

and brushing my teeth.

When I wanted to play with my toys,
it sat on me.

It even made me stay indoors when my friends came to play . . .

I wanted to go out and join them, but my monster
stood in the way and wouldn't budge.

One day, my monster was
waiting for me after school.

It was **GIGANTIC** and it was in a bad mood.

I tried to lose it . . . but I couldn't.

It followed me all the way to Gran's house.

Gran asked me what was wrong.

In the end, I told her how my monster just wouldn't go away.
It **WOULDN'T** leave me alone. **Ever**.

Gran listened quietly . . .

. . . and **suddenly** my monster stopped what it was doing and listened too. It seemed to me that as I talked, my monster got smaller . . .

and smaller . . .

and smaller . . .

And then I knew that I **COULD** make my monster go away.

The next day, I saw my monster at school.

It looked a bit lost,
so I picked it up and
put it in my pocket.

I stroked its fur and it went to sleep.

It wasn't as **SCARY** any more.

I don't worry about my monster so much these days.
I go to school and play with my friends.

My **MONSTER** likes my pocket
and I feel OK knowing it's there.

But if it ever
feels like
getting out,
I tell it
to behave.

My monster is part of me.
We've known each other from the beginning.

This is **me**.

And this is my monster.